Shamrock's
Cursed Hoof

Also by Daisy Sunshine

Twilight, Say Cheese!
Sapphire's Special Power
Shamrock's Seaside Sleepover
Comet's Big Win
Twilight's Grand Finale
Sapphire's Summer Disguise

UNICORN
University

#7

Shamrock's
Cursed Hoof

★ by DAISY SUNSHINE ★
illustrated by MONIQUE DONG

ALADDIN
New York London Toronto Sydney New Delhi

ALADDIN

An imprint of Simon & Schuster Children's Publishing Division

1230 Avenue of the Americas, New York, New York 10020

First Aladdin hardcover edition October 2022

Text copyright © 2022 by Simon & Schuster, Inc.

Illustrations copyright © 2022 by Monique Dong

Also available in an Aladdin paperback edition.

All rights reserved, including the right of reproduction in whole or in part in any form.

ALADDIN and related logo are registered trademarks of Simon & Schuster, Inc.

For information about special discounts for bulk purchases, please contact Simon & Schuster Special Sales at 1-866-506-1949 or business@simonandschuster.com.

The Simon & Schuster Speakers Bureau can bring authors to your live event. For more information or to book an event contact the Simon & Schuster Speakers Bureau at 1-866-248-3049 or visit our website at www.simonspeakers.com.

Book designed by Laura Lyn DiSiena

The illustrations for this book were rendered digitally.

The text of this book was set in Tinos.

Manufactured in the United States of America 0922 FFG

2 4 6 8 10 9 7 5 3 1

Library of Congress Cataloging-in-Publication Data

Names: Sunshine, Daisy, author. | Dong, Monique, illustrator. Title: Shamrock's cursed hoof / by Daisy Sunshine ; illustrated by Monique Dong.

Description: First Aladdin paperback edition. | New York : Aladdin, 2022. |

Series: Unicorn university | "Also available in an Aladdin hardcover edition." | Summary: Shamrock is excited to study garden science, but when his Golden Rose seed does not grow, he becomes convinced that he has the Gardener's Curse and only a secret visit to Doctor Mush in the Gnome Village will help.

Identifiers: LCCN 2022008111 (print) | LCCN 2022008112 (ebook) |

ISBN 9781665901048 (hardcover) | ISBN 9781665901031 (paperback) | ISBN 9781665901055 (ebook)

Subjects: LCSH: Unicorns—Juvenile fiction. | Gnomes—Juvenile fiction. | Gardening—Juvenile fiction. | Blessing and cursing—Juvenile fiction. | Friendship—Juvenile fiction. | Helping behavior—Juvenile fiction. | CYAC: Unicorns—Fiction. | Gnomes—Fiction. | Gardening—Fiction. | Blessing and cursing—Fiction. | Friendship—Fiction. | Helpfulness—Fiction. | LCGFT: Novels.

Classification: LCC PZ7.1.S867 Se 2022 (print) | LCC PZ7.1.S867 (ebook) | DDC [Fic]—dc23

LC record available at https://lccn.loc.gov/2022008111

LC ebook record available at https://lccn.loc.gov/2022008112

For lovers of sparkles, rainbows, and magic

CONTENTS

1

Greenhouse Greetings

S hamrock felt the spring air brush his cheek as he made his way across the Friendly Fields of Unicorn University. The tall grasses swayed, and the few clouds in the sky looked like huge wispy feathers. It was a chilly afternoon, and his glasses clouded over as he breathed. He wondered why his lenses always fogged up like that in the cold, and he made a mental note to look it up in the library later.

Science was always Shamrock's favorite subject at Unicorn University. He loved studying and learning about the ways things worked, even out of the classroom.

Potions had to be his favorite class of all, though—he loved following each step in the process to create something magical. But it was a new semester, and instead of Potions class, he had Garden Science. He and his classmates would learn all about magical plants in the five kingdoms—and how to grow them! Shamrock was really excited. He had read the textbook, *Gardening 101*, last night and couldn't wait to start studying different plants.

Once he reached the edge of the Friendly Fields, Shamrock found himself at the greenhouse, where Garden Science class was held. The structure looked like a house made of big glass windows, even on the roof. Shamrock had read in his textbook that the windows let lots of sunshine in during the day and then trapped the heat inside after sunset, when the air outside cooled down.

He pushed open the door and felt like he was entering another world. The air was warm and a little sticky, and the whole room smelled like soil. Which made sense, as there were plants growing everywhere! Different kinds of plants of every size and color and shape, from a crinkly-leafed fern to a bright pink sunflower.

Looking around, Shamrock realized he was the first student there. He always like to be early on the first day so he could pick his spot and get ready. Searching around the room, he found the perfect table in the corner. It was big—perfect for him and his three best friends—and seemed like the cleanest one, although there were still a few clumps of dirt and empty pots scattered about. Shamrock thought back to his Potions class, with its clean tables and shelves of glass bottles with their neat labels. He had to admit, he liked his neat Potions classroom better. Shamrock liked to be organized, and there was something about this messy greenhouse that made him feel a little squirmy.

As Shamrock settled in, other students started to arrive, and soon the greenhouse was filled with the sounds of unicorns chatting and laughing. Shamrock's friends Comet,

Sapphire, and Twilight came in and sat by him.

"Wow," Twilight said softly. She was gazing around in awe. "This place is magical. I wonder if this is how fairies feel in gardens." With a hoof that was painted bright green, she pointed to some of the bigger plants that hung from the ceiling. Her green hoof stood out against her jet-black coat but blended into the plants all around them. Shamrock wondered if she'd chosen to paint her hooves green just for Garden Science class.

"I know what you mean!" Comet said. "It feels like we shrank down to tiny unicorns. A lot of these plants are bigger than us!" Comet whipped her short, cropped mane around to look behind her—almost knocking a potted plant down in the process.

Sapphire reached a bright blue hoof over to catch the pot just in time and pushed it back onto its table.

She chuckled. "I have no idea what you guys are talking about. But it is cool in here!"

Shamrock was with Sapphire. Comet and Twilight were the artists in their group and sometimes spoke in their own dreamy language. Twilight was a painter, and Comet was an artist at baking pastries.

"I'm pretty excited about this class," Twilight told them. "Growing up on a farm, I learned a lot from my parents about gardening, so I feel . . . well, I guess I feel confident?"

Comet laughed. "Yay, Twilight! You totally should. You're the only one in our stable who has kept a plant alive in her stall. You'll be great."

Shamrock nodded in agreement. He was happy to see his friend feeling so confident. Twilight could be shy, and she didn't always believe in herself as much as she should.

"Well, actually . . ." Peppermint, a snow-white unicorn with a red-and-white-striped mane, leaned over from her table to theirs. "I heard that the garden professor is super scary and loves pop quizzes!"

Shamrock smiled. "That would be all right! I've already

studied the intro to gardening book the professor assigned. I would ace any quiz."

"I love that attitude!" The whole class turned to where a dark green unicorn stood in the corner of the greenhouse. Her horn was covered in dirt, and there were leaves tangled in her long green mane. At first glance she looked like another one of the plants! Shamrock wondered how long she had been there without anyone noticing. He felt embarrassed about bragging now.

The dark green unicorn stepped into the light. The whole class could see she was smiling wide. Shamrock thought she seemed friendly, but with all that dirt he didn't think she looked much like a scientist. His potions professor always wore a clean white lab coat.

"I'm Professor Grub," she told the class. "And I hope by the end of this class you'll all love the magic of gardening as much as I do." On the table in front of her was a jar filled with what looked like hundreds of pebbles of different shapes and sizes. She pushed the jar over so the pebbles spilled onto the wooden table. Using her hoof, she spread them out. Shamrock realized that they were seeds, and that each one was different. Some were big and round, but some were so tiny that you had to squint to see them. "Each one of these seeds has the potential to grow into something amazing. They are filled with magic—and we can help that magic flourish by planting and caring for them. That is what garden science is all about."

Shamrock tilted his head, feeling puzzled. This was not the way he was used to talking about science. But as he looked around, he saw that most of the class was inspired by her words. Everyone was smiling and looking at the tiny pebbles as if they were fairy dust. Comet and Twilight were especially entranced.

"For your first homework assignment," Professor Grub started to say next, "I want you each to find a seed you'd like to grow over the next few months. Think about your own life and interests, what kind of flower you would want to grow, and why."

Homework was something Shamrock enjoyed, but growing something already? Didn't they need to learn more first?

Shamrock's classmates started excitedly talking to one another about what kind of plants they'd like to grow. To his

right, Sapphire was mentioning aloe, and Comet seemed set on daisies. But Shamrock scrunched his eyebrows, feeling a little worried. Had he missed an assignment? He hadn't studied seeds yet. He had focused on the parts of a plant and the climate they lived in here in Sunshine Springs. So how could he know which would be the perfect seed to grow?

Shamrock worried he was already behind. This was a new feeling, and he did not like it one bit.

2

Super Seeds

When the hour was up, Shamrock followed his friends out of the greenhouse. He breathed in the cool spring air, which made him feel a little better. It was muggy in that greenhouse. Maybe that was why he was feeling confused.

"What does everyone want to plant?" Twilight asked. The wind swirled around, making her long black mane blow in the wind.

"I was thinking of growing this plant my grandmother always used to grow," Sapphire told them. "When you cut it open, you can use the special goo inside to help heal cuts. I've been learning a new hoofball move, and I keep falling and getting scrapes. I've been wishing I had some of it around!"

Shamrock adjusted his bag and couldn't help but feel jealous. That was a really cool idea!

"I was reading a cookbook the other night for fun—" Comet started to say, but she stopped when all her friends began laughing. They could never understand how someone

could read a cookbook for fun! Comet grinned and waved them away with her hoof. "*Anyway*, I was reading the cookbook, and a recipe said you could decorate a cake with these edible flowers. What if I grew flowers for the baking competition? That would wow the judges for sure!"

That was a really good idea too! Comet had won a baking competition against Glitterhorn College, and now she was getting ready for an even bigger baking competition at the capital. If Shamrock were a judge, he would be impressed by a baker growing their very own decorations.

"I love that," Twilight said. "There are some plants you can turn into dye for paints, too. I've been working on a painting of the Spotlight Flowers. I wonder if I could grow one and then make a dye out of it!"

Shamrock was so impressed by his friends. They had already thought of awesome plants to grow. But he couldn't think of anything. What would show off his science skills best? What would get him an A+? He had no idea.

Shamrock *always* had great ideas for class projects. He didn't know why Garden Science felt so different.

"What about you, Shamrock?" Twilight asked.

Shamrock felt his cheeks get red. Not wanting to admit that he was feeling stumped, he just said, "It's going to be a surprise! My plant is going to be something no one has ever seen before. It's really special." A little knot grew in his stomach. He didn't like lying to his friends. But they expected him to be awesome at everything involving science, and he didn't want to let them down.

"Leave it to Shamrock!" Comet said.

"I can't wait to see it!" Twilight told him.

Shamrock felt the knot in his stomach grow even bigger. He tried to make himself feel better by telling himself that he really would find the perfect surprise seed. Once he found it, he wouldn't be lying anymore!

"I'm going to head to the library to get started on research for the project," Shamrock said as he broke off from the group and turned toward the glittering library. "I'll see you all later!"

As he trotted off, Shamrock told himself that he had a good plan. It would all come together in the library. Things always made sense there.

3

Dr. Mush

S hamrock? Shamrock?"

Shamrock lifted his horn to see Professor Jazz, the librarian, staring back at him. Looking around the library, Shamrock realized that the whole place was empty. Only Shamrock and his stacks of gardening books were left.

"What time is it?" Shamrock asked.

"Time to get out of here!" Professor Jazz told him with a smile. "I rang the closing bell, but you just slept right through it! Which is impressive. The bell is pretty loud, and a hundred unicorns all walking on the library's crystal floors sound like a thunderstorm. I'm glad I caught you on my walk-through, or you would have been stuck here all night."

Shamrock blinked at the librarian with surprise. Then, looking at his stack of books, he felt his heart drop. He had looked through the whole gardening section and still hadn't found the perfect amazing plant that he had promised his friends.

"What are you looking for?" Professor Jazz asked. "Maybe I can help."

"It's for Garden Science," Shamrock explained. "I need to find the perfect seed. It has to be something no one has ever heard of before. It needs to be extraordinary!"

Professor Jazz nodded his head, his long shaggy mane swaying with each nod. Then he looked up with a sparkle in his eye. "I think I have just the right book!"

Shamrock wasn't so sure. "I've already looked through all your gardening books, Professor. I didn't find what I was looking for."

"Oh, but this is not a gardening book. It's a journal!"

Shamrock was confused. Was Professor Jazz not listening? He needed information on plants! Not someone's journal!

"Wait right here." Professor Jazz turned quickly and disappeared down one of the rows of books. When he came back, a book was hanging from his horn by its ring. The book was small and thin, and the cover looked a little dirty. Shamrock didn't think it looked very impressive.

"Don't judge a book by its cover!" Professor Jazz told Shamrock upon seeing the look on his face. "This is the journal of Dr. Mush, a world-renowned plant scientist and gnome who lives right here in Sunshine Springs. In fact, he lives in the gnome village not too far from Unicorn University and often comes to visit for a cup of tea! We're old friends, and I can tell you he is brilliant and knows more about rare plants than anyone else in the five kingdoms. This journal was a gift from him. I'm sure you'll find some inspiration in it."

Shamrock's heart soared. This seemed like just what he needed! Now that he'd heard Professor Jazz's praise, the slim book looked much more important. "You were right, Professor. I was judging a book by its cover. But this is the perfect thing!"

Professor Jazz smiled. "I'm so happy I could help. Now off you go to bed, Shamrock!"

Shamrock smiled and stood, and only then realized that he was really sleepy. He pushed the journal into his schoolbag and headed to his stable for bed.

But when he got to his stall, having passed all of his sleeping classmates, Shamrock didn't feel like lying down. He wanted to look through Dr. Mush's journal. Just to see what the doctor might have to say.

The lights were off in the barn, so Shamrock turned on his flashlight and opened to the first page. It was filled with detailed drawings of strange and unusual plants, as well as descriptions and little tips for caring for them. All of the pages were filled with drawings and descriptions! And in between notes on plants, Dr. Mush described his travels through the five kingdoms. He talked of how he'd learned about different plants from all over the world, what they were used for, and how to grow them. It was fascinating.

Shamrock kept reading and reading, even though he knew he should get to bed if he wanted to be awake and

alert for his classes tomorrow. But before he knew it, he was at the very last page! There, next to a drawing of a large flowering plant with oddly shaped leaves and huge petals, Dr. Mush had written, "The Golden Rose is the biggest flower I've ever seen or heard of. It's so bright and shiny, it feels like you've harvested the sun."

Shamrock smiled. He'd found it! The Golden Rose would be spectacular. He knew he would wow the class with his choice.

4

The Perfect Flower

Shamrock blinked open his eyes in the morning, woken up by the hustle and bustle of students getting ready for class. Despite not having gotten much sleep, Shamrock was awake and excited about the day. He packed Dr. Mush's journal in his bag and headed out of the stables. He couldn't wait for Garden Science so he could tell everyone about the seed he'd picked.

Finally the afternoon came, and Shamrock pushed open the glass doors of the greenhouse. This time he wasn't the first one to class. Unicorns were already gathered around their wooden tables, and everyone seemed to be talking about their seeds. But Shamrock felt confident that no one would have picked a seed like his. He settled next to Twilight at their table and pulled out Dr. Mush's journal by the horn ring.

Professor Grub called for the class to quiet down. "Let's start by sharing which seeds everyone has chosen. We'll go around, and each student can name which plant they're going to grow over the next few months."

The professor glanced up and looked around the room. All of the students' horns rose a little higher with excitement.

"Let's start with you, Peppermint," Professor Grub said, turning to her right.

Starting with Peppermint, who pledged to grow Rainbow Roses, each student named the plant they'd chosen. Shamrock was amazed by all the different seeds—and all the different things they grew into. From food for unicorns to houses for pixies.

It seemed to take forever to get around to his table, but soon Twilight announced her plan to use Spotlight Flowers to create dye for paint, and it was Shamrock's turn. He was the last one to go. Shamrock couldn't help but wiggle with happiness.

"I discovered this seed when I was reading Dr. Mush's journal. He's a famous scientist. He finds super-rare and strange plants all over the five kingdoms and discovered the Golden Rose, which shines like the sun. And that's what I'm going to grow."

The whole class oohed and aahed. Shamrock smiled, feeling like he'd won a competition.

Professor Grub scrunched her eyebrows a little. "It is a very impressive flower, Shamrock. But it is very difficult to grow."

Shamrock puffed his chest out. "It's okay, I'm up to the challenge. Science is kind of my thing."

"He's right!" one student shouted from the back. "If

anyone can grow a super-strange flower, Shamrock can. He's the smartest kid in our class."

The rest of the students murmured in agreement. Shamrock blushed. He was so happy, he felt like he was floating on air.

"Ah," Professor Grub said. "Well, we shall see, won't we! Okay, then, let's get to work! Everyone get a pot and some soil I have over here. I used a little of my magic on it to speed up the growing process. That way we can all have our plants growing before long. I'll go to our storage shed and get the seeds you requested. The seed packets will have instructions to help guide you. Happy growing, all!"

As Professor Grub left the greenhouse, Shamrock went to get his pot and his soil, and brought them back to his spot at the wooden table.

Professor Grub soon returned with the seeds, and she began handing them out. Before long she was standing before Shamrock. "Here you are, Shamrock. Golden Rose seeds are very rare, but luckily, Dr. Mush gave me some the last time he stopped by for a visit with Professor Jazz. He even wrote down instructions."

Thrilled, Shamrock looked at the handwritten paper that was covered with dirt splotches. The writing looked just like the writing in Dr. Mush's journal. Shamrock was amazed. He would be growing Dr. Mush's own seeds and following the doctor's own directions. Shamrock's rose was going to be the best plant in the class for sure!

"Just let me know if you need any help," Professor Grub told him before walking over to the next student.

Shamrock nodded, barely hearing her, as he had already started studying Dr. Mush's directions.

At the very top the first note read, "Fill a tiny pot with soil. Pack down with your hoof three times."

Shamrock got to work filling up the pot with soil and packed it down with his hoof three times, just like the doctor had written.

"Hey, Shamrock?"

Shamrock looked up to see Twilight staring at his pot full of soil. "Yes, Twilight?" he asked.

"I think you might be packing the soil in a little too tight. It's important for the soil to be loose, so that the seedling can grow."

Shamrock just shook his head. "Nope. Dr. Mush says right here to pack it three times."

"Oh, you're probably right, then." Twilight smiled and went back to her pot of soil.

"Want to use some of my super-top-secret gardening fertilizer my grandmother always uses?" Comet asked him a few minutes later. "I told her in my letter that I was taking Garden Science, and she mailed me three jars."

Shamrock shook his head again. "Nope. There's nothing about fertilizer in the directions."

Comet turned to Twilight to see if she needed any of the fertilizer.

"Shamrock—" Sapphire said.

Shamrock couldn't help but be annoyed. He was trying to work! "Yes?" he asked in a way that was not very nice. He didn't mean to be rude, but he didn't understand why everyone kept bothering him!

"I was only going to say that my mom always says that the best gardeners work with other gardeners. You have to help each other out with the tricks you've learned along the way!"

Shamrock shook his head again. "That might be true for growing food for your garden, but this is a *very special* flower. Professor Grub even said it was hard to grow. I think I'll just stick to the directions that Dr. Mush wrote here."

Sapphire shrugged and went back to planting her own seeds.

Without further distractions Shamrock planted his seeds just the way Dr. Mush had written out.

After finishing the last step, he very carefully pushed

the potted plant over to the sunniest corner of the table. Dr. Mush had said that the Golden Rose needed lots and lots of sunlight. Shamrock smiled at the little pot and imagined the rose it would soon house. Satisfied, he stepped away from the table just as class ended.

Back at the stables later, Shamrock looked into a mirror and was surprised to find he had dirt all over his glasses and a smudge on his nose. Now he understood why Professor Grub didn't wear a clean white coat like his Potions professor did.

Shamrock went to bed excited, and as he slept, he dreamt of growing the world's best Golden Rose.

5

A Stubborn Seedling

The next week, Shamrock was eating lunch under the twisty apple trees when he overheard two unicorns from Garden Science excitedly chatting. Their plants had started to sprout!

When it was time for class, Shamrock hurried to check on his Golden Rose. But when he got to the greenhouse, he was disappointed to find that the soil in his pot still looked the same as it had on the day when he'd planted the seed. There wasn't anything growing yet that he could see. He bit his lip and looked around at the other pots, only to find that almost all the other students did have tiny green plants popping above dark brown soil.

Except for his.

"Now that our seeds have begun to sprout," Professor Grub said to the class, "what can we observe?"

Twilight raised her hand.

"Yes, Twilight?" Professor Grub asked.

Very softly Twilight replied, "Even though we all planted different things, our plants look a lot alike so far. Most of them are tiny green plants with two little leaves."

"Very good, Twilight." Professor Grub smiled. "Right now these little plants are called seedlings."

Professor Grub kept talking, but Shamrock couldn't focus for the rest of class. He didn't have a seedling yet! He looked back at Dr. Mush's directions and tried to figure out what step he'd missed. But he'd followed the directions exactly.

After class Shamrock walked over to Professor Grub as she checked on a large, strange spiky plant in the corner.

A little embarrassed, Shamrock hung his horn. He wasn't used to feeling behind in class.

"Professor Grub?" he asked, his voice squeaking a little at the end.

Professor Grub looked up with a smile. "Yes, Shamrock?"

"I was wondering about my plant. . . . It hasn't sprouted like the rest, even though I followed all the instructions perfectly."

Professor Grub nodded. "I believe I mentioned that the Golden Rose is known for being hard to grow. Why don't you plant another flower, like a red rose, too? Then you can compare the two and perhaps learn about the Golden Rose along the way."

Shamrock felt a pang in his chest. Did the professor

think he couldn't do it? His eyebrows scrunched so low, they started to disappear behind his glasses.

"You might want to talk to Peppermint too," Professor Grub suggested. "She's been growing Rainbow Roses, which are in the same plant family as the Golden Rose. Maybe she has some advice."

Shamrock felt his cheeks grow warm. This professor must have thought he was the worst in the whole class if he already needed so much help! And Shamrock was always the *best* in his classes. He never needed to ask anyone for help. Especially not another student.

Shamrock could only nod in response. He didn't want to be rude, but he didn't want to cry, either. He turned on his hoof and ran right to his stable. He got out the intro to gardening textbook and studied it from front to back until the sky was dark and he was yawning, only pausing to eat a quick dinner. He would show the professor that he could be just as good at garden science as Peppermint.

6

Saturday Blues

It was Saturday and there were no classes, but Shamrock headed to the greenhouses first thing in the morning to check on his plant. It had been a week since his talk with Professor Grub, and so far there was no tiny plant in his pot. Shamrock had studied all the gardening books and tried *everything* to make it grow. He'd moved the plant to different parts of the room for more sunlight. He'd watered it at different times of day. He'd even wrapped the pot in a scarf to keep it warm.

But nothing had worked.

Even so, it was a new day, and Shamrock was hopeful as he entered the greenhouse. But all that hope disappeared when he stopped in front of his pot. There was not even a speck of green life growing. Just dirt. Dirty brown dirt.

Embarrassed, disappointed, and alone in the greenhouse, he pulled out Dr. Grub's journal and flipped through the old pages, each crinkling as he turned it. He studied the entry on the Golden Rose. Maybe there was a clue to help him figure out the mystery of the plant. He reread the part about how beautiful the Golden Rose was, how it was the loveliest rose Dr. Grub had ever seen. He studied again the margins that were filled with drawings of each stage of the plant. There was the pot with soil, a sketch of the little seedling, and all the stages before it became the huge flower that was bigger than a unicorn. As Shamrock looked closely at the page, he noticed some writing squished on the side, written along the book's edge. He turned the book sideways and peered more closely, his glasses almost touching the page.

His heart skipped a beat when he read, "Beware of the Gardener's Curse!"

7

The Gardener's Curse

Shamrock felt his stomach drop. *Do I have the Gardener's Curse? Is that why I can't grow the Golden Rose?*

He looked more closely at the page. Under the warning, Dr. Mush had written, "If you can't get your plant to grow, no matter what you try, you may have been cursed. The only cure is—"

Shamrock groaned. The rest of the writing was smeared, so he couldn't read it!

Shamrock knew in his heart that he had the Gardener's Curse. Why else would he be the only one in class who couldn't get his plant to grow? The only question was, how could he get rid of the curse and still get an A+ in Garden Science, especially if the cure wasn't in the journal?

Shamrock wandered away from the greenhouse, leaving his pot of soil behind. All he could think about was the curse. How had he gotten it? And how did he get rid of it? As he walked through the bright green grass, he couldn't help but stare at his hooves and worry. If he had the Gardener's Curse, then he'd never be able to grow a Golden Rose with his own two hooves.

He was so lost in thought that he hardly knew where his cursed hooves were taking him. Then he found himself outside Stella and Celest's cabin. Stella and Celest were the school chefs, and they made all the Unicorn University food and treats there. Stella and Celest might have been chefs for the whole school, but Shamrock and his friends always felt like the cabin with the big kitchen was their own special place. A stone chimney was always puffing out little gray clouds of smoke, and the most delicious smells were constantly wafting out of the open windows.

Feeling heartened, Shamrock pushed open their round red door to find Stella, a dragon, looking through a magnifying glass at a large cookbook filled with lots and lots of tiny writing. The old wooden table was covered in tissues, and a steaming cup of tea sat next to the cookbook.

"Hey, Stella," Shamrock said as he closed the door behind him.

"Hey, Shamrock!" Stella said. "Where are your best pals?"

Shamrock shrugged. "I had to do some research this morning."

Stella smiled. "Me too. I've been thinking about this soup my grandmother used to make when I was small, but I can't find the recipe anywhere. She made it for me when I had a cold, and it always made me feel better. And as you can see, I have a cold right now and could really use some of that soup!" Stella waved her arm over the evidence on the table.

"Is there anything I can do to help?" Shamrock asked.

She just shook her head. "Not unless you know how to make this soup."

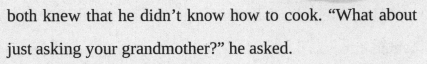

Shamrock smiled. They both knew that he didn't know how to cook. "What about just asking your grandmother?" he asked.

"She died a few years back, sadly," she said, blinking back tears. "And my mom doesn't know where the recipe is either. I fear it might be lost!"

"What about someone else in your family?" he asked.

Stella looked up quickly with a grin. "You know, that's not a bad idea! I could ask my cousins. Maybe one of them has it!"

Shamrock nodded. "I hope you feel better soon, Stella."

He headed for the door so that she could get some rest.

"Thanks, Shamrock!" Stella said behind him. "Always good to remember to keep asking for help. Even if you don't get the right answer on the first try."

Shamrock thought about what Stella had said as he walked away from the school kitchens. He wasn't really sure where to go for help with the Golden Rose. He'd already asked Professor Grub, and she'd basically told him that he was a lost cause. He'd already looked through all the gardening books the library had, so Professor Jazz couldn't help either. Who else could he ask? Shamrock had to admit that he felt, well . . . helpless. He just didn't know what to do.

On the way back to the stables, he thought, *I wish I could talk to Dr. Mush. He would know how to cure the curse.*

Then, as if a lightbulb had turned on in his brain, Shamrock realized he really could talk to Dr. Mush. Hadn't Professor Jazz said that the doctor lived in the gnome village in the forest by Unicorn University?

Using his magical memory—his special ability—Shamrock thought of the map he'd studied of Unicorn University and the lands around it. Picturing the landscape in his mind, Shamrock knew he would be able to walk to the gnome village and back before the end of the day. No one would even notice he was gone.

Shamrock also knew the school handbook by heart, and he knew that it was against the rules to leave school grounds. And Shamrock always followed the rules. Well, almost always.

The part of Shamrock that wanted to get an A+ in Garden Science told him to run to the gnome village and get rid of the curse. But the part of him that didn't want to get in trouble told him to stay put at Unicorn University. Shamrock groaned. He was giving himself a headache.

When he got to his stall in the stable, he pulled out a notebook to write a list. That always helped him make big decisions.

Reasons not to go see Dr. Mush: He'd get expelled and not be able to see his friends again. His dads would be mad.

Reasons to go see Dr. Mush: He'd remove the curse, get an A+ in Garden Science, and feel like himself again.

Shamrock stared at his list. His bushy eyebrows scrunched behind his glasses as he puzzled over it. Then he remembered Stella's words of wisdom and wrote them down on the "Reasons to Go" list: "It's always a good idea to keep asking for help."

Mathematically speaking, the "Reasons to Go" list did have more points, Shamrock noticed. He made his decision. He was going into the forest in search of Dr. Mush.

With that, Shamrock pulled down his backpack to fill with supplies. The forest was no Friendly Fields. It was filled with dangerous magic, and the road to the gnome village was long and winding. Shamrock first packed his flashlight, then the chocolates his dads had sent him in their last care package. He grabbed a sweater in case it got cool, and finally a rope. He had read once that it was always a good idea to carry rope.

Squaring his shoulders and throwing his backpack over his shoulder, Shamrock headed out of the stables, ready for the deep, dark woods. But before he could get any farther, he ran into three familiar faces, all of them looking puzzled.

Uh-oh.

8

Into the Forest

Twilight, Sapphire, and Comet stood in front of Shamrock and stared at the big pack he was carrying.

"Where ya going, Sham?" Comet asked, with a sparkle in her eye. No one else could spot mischief like Comet.

"Is everything okay?" Twilight asked him, her own eyes twinkling with worry.

And finally Sapphire added, "Is this about Garden Science?"

Shamrock could only gape at his friend. How did Sapphire always know exactly what was going on?

"Well, wherever you're going," Comet chimed in, "we're obviously coming with you to help."

Sapphire nodded with a smile, and even Twilight said, "Of course."

Shamrock just shook his head. He couldn't let them break the rules, even if he was going to. "No way, guys. I'm going" —he looked from side to side to make sure no one was looking, and dropped his voice to a whisper—"to the woods. I have to find Dr. Mush. He lives in the gnome village."

"Of course we'll come," Comet said. "I have always wanted to explore the woods!"

"You'll need help in the woods. They're supposed to be super scary, and you'll need backup," Sapphire said with so much confidence that she sounded like a teacher.

Twilight tilted her head in confusion. "But why do you need to find Dr. Mush, Shamrock?"

Shamrock stared at his hooves, heart pounding. He had no idea what his friends would think.

After scraping the grass with his hoof a few times, Shamrock took a deep breath and admitted the truth. "I have the Gardener's Curse. That's why I can't grow the Golden Rose." He pulled out Dr. Mush's journal, laid it open on the ground between them, and flipped to the right page. He pointed his hoof at the cramped note. "See? It says, 'Beware of the Gardener's Curse! No one can grow the Golden Rose when the curse is upon them.' These hooves are cursed. *I'm* cursed!"

His three best friends stared back at him with their jaws hanging open, their eyes wide with surprise.

"You know, I was wondering why your plant was the only one not to sprout yet," Sapphire said first. "Science is always your best class!"

Comet nodded, her short blond mane bobbing as she did. "If you need to do this, Shamrock, we've got your back. Should we stop by Stella and Celest's cabin and get some snacks for the road?"

Twilight sighed a little. "Are we sure the curse is real? Have you asked Professor Grub for help? And what about Professor Jazz? Won't we be breaking the rules by going into the forest?"

Shamrock bounced a little from hoof to hoof, feeling nervous. "The handbook says we aren't allowed to leave school grounds . . . but I did go to Professor Grub! She didn't even tell me about the curse. And I've already looked through all the library's gardening books, and there's *nothing* about the Gardener's Curse. So I'm not sure how Professor Jazz could help either."

"It's decided, then," Twilight said, her voice quiet but serious. "We're going into the forest. But no snacks," she said, looking at Comet. "We have to make this fast."

With Twilight in, the four friends squared their shoulders and made their way across the Friendly Fields, past the Pleasant Pastures, and over the Bubbling Brook. But they paused at the entrance to the dark woods.

"Okay," Shamrock said, his voice a little higher than usual. "Once we step into the woods, we're officially leaving Unicorn University."

Twilight gulped. "And officially breaking school rules. I hope no one will be too mad at us."

"They can only be mad if they find out," Comet said, leaping into the woods ahead of them.

Sapphire looked at Shamrock and Twilight and shrugged. "I guess we'd better go after her."

Twilight and Shamrock watched Sapphire's blue tail disappear behind a scraggly tree.

"Together?" Twilight asked, her voice just above a whisper.

"Together," Shamrock agreed. And the two of them stepped into the woods.

The trees reached high into the sky, with leaves and branches twisting to form a ceiling above them. Only small dots of sunlight trickled down to the winding dirt path.

Shamrock shuddered when he heard something howl in the distance. The path was so narrow that they had to walk single file. No one dared to utter a word as the unicorns walked along the path for what felt like hours. Shamrock kept his head down and focused on putting one hoof in front of the other.

"Agh!" Comet screamed from her spot at the front of the group. Shamrock whipped his head up and tried to see where Comet had gone. But he couldn't see her anywhere. He started to sweat, worried something had pulled her into the forest.

"She's up there!" Sapphire motioned with her horn, pointing above them.

Shamrock's stomach dropped into his hooves when he saw Comet, stuck in a giant spiderweb that was hung between two trees. He had never seen a spiderweb so big! He went cold when he realized how big a spider would have to be to spin a web that big.

"Ugh, gross," Comet whined. She tried to move her legs in the sticky threads, but they were held tight.

"How'd you end up there?" Twilight asked, her voice squeaky with worry.

Sapphire shook her head. "I told her not to do it! She wanted to fly up and see how much farther the gnome village was. But then—well—she got stuck."

Comet groaned. "Yeah, yeah. You were right, as usual."

"Well, can you see the gnome village?" Shamrock asked. He felt like they'd been walking for a long time. The map said they just had to follow this path all the way. But it had felt much longer than it had looked.

Comet shook her head. "Nope, nothing but trees. Now can we figure out a way to get me down from here?"

"I have a rope in my bag!" Shamrock told them, pulling out the long cord. He knew he'd need it someday!

"But how do we get it to her?" Twilight asked, her eyebrows scrunched as she looked up to Comet.

"Let's tie it around this stick. Then Comet can hold on to the stick with her teeth," Shamrock said, thinking quickly. *I got them into this mess,* he thought, *so I'd better be able to get them out.*

"I'll kick the stick up to you, Comet!" Sapphire said. "Just like we're at hoofball practice."

"And I'll tie the other end of the rope around my horn. If I run fast, I can pull you out of the web," Shamrock told them, excited that they were figuring it out. "Simple science."

"Then I can fly down to the ground! Once you pull me out of these sticky threads."

Soon everything was ready to go. One side of the rope was tied to the stick, and the other end was tied to Shamrock's horn.

"Ready, Comet?" Sapphire asked. The stick with the rope tied to it was on the ground in front of her.

"Ready!" Comet said, ready to catch the stick with her mouth.

Sapphire backed up, then ran forward and kicked the stick with her front hoof. The four unicorns watched it fly up and up and arch right over to Comet. Comet shifted a little and caught it! They all cheered with relief.

"Wish Coach could've seen that," Sapphire said, her eyes glittering with the win.

Shamrock smiled. "My turn! Hold on to that stick, Comet."

Shamrock broke into a run, pulling the rope as much as he could. The rope went slack, and he looked behind him to see Comet pulled free from the web, but—oh no!—she was flying right into a tree, not onto the path! Comet hit a large tree trunk with a big *thump* and tumbled down to the ground. Her friends went running over.

"Ouch," she said as she looked up through sticky spiderweb threads that had gotten caught in her mane. "Help me up?"

Her friends pulled her to her hooves, but Comet groaned

as she put one of her back hooves on the ground. "Uh-oh," she said. "I think I twisted my ankle."

"Can you still fly?" Shamrock asked quickly, worried that their mission would end before he got any answers about the curse.

Comet shook her head. "I need my hooves to fly—it's kind of like swimming. I think we need to turn back." Comet tried limping on her three legs. She could move slowly, but it was clear she needed help. "I don't think we'll make it to the gnome village and back before dark, going this slowly. I'm sorry, Shamrock."

"Of course," Sapphire said. "Let's help you get back."

"Can you lean on us?" Twilight asked.

Twilight and Sapphire stood on either side of Comet, holding her up between them.

"I'm sorry, Shamrock," Comet said again as she limped with the others back toward school.

Shamrock bit his lip. He could feel his heart pounding

in his chest. "Listen, you all head back. I'm going to keep going."

Sapphire shook her head. She had her super-serious face on. "No way, Shamrock. You shouldn't be in this forest alone. And Comet needs our help."

But Shamrock had his stubborn face on, and he wasn't going to budge. "I'm sorry, but this is something I have to do." And before they could say anything else, he broke into a run toward the gnome village, knowing they couldn't follow him. *I hope they won't be too mad*, he thought. *But this curse needs to be broken. Comet has to see a healer for her ankle, and I have to see Dr. Mush about my curse.*

9

Going Gnome

Shamrock ran deeper and deeper into the dark forest. The path grew narrower as he traveled, and branches seemed to reach out to him, getting tangled in his mane. The path stretched on forever, with no sign of the gnome village. Shamrock started to doubt his magic memory. Was he wrong about the map? Maybe he should just turn back and find his friends.

But then Shamrock heard a guitar in the distance. And were those voices singing?

Shamrock slowed down to a walk and followed the

music. Soon he heard the sounds of carts being pulled and horses neighing. *The gnome village!* he thought with joy. Shamrock continued to follow the village sounds until he stood in front of the biggest tree he had ever seen. It had little windows all around the giant trunk. Through the windows he could see little red pointed hats bouncing inside. *Finally*, he thought, *I've made it!*

Shamrock walked by the giant tree and found himself in the center of a small grove of very tall trees. Bridges made from rope hung between the trees, and each trunk had a round red door at its base. Gnomes of all ages and beard lengths walked among the trees. Some pushed carts full of carrots half their size. Some carried large piles of scrolls. And some just sat at tables, laughing and talking with other gnomes. Shamrock even spotted the band he had heard in the woods. A group of gnomes with instruments was sitting on a large mushroom, singing together.

But it wasn't long before all the gnomes in the village stopped what they were doing to stare at Shamrock. He gulped, realizing that he was there uninvited. Not to mention that he had snuck away from school without telling a teacher. Suddenly his great plan did not seem so great after all.

"How can we help you, young lad?" the gnome with the guitar finally asked, breaking the silence.

Shamrock smiled, grateful someone else had said

something first. "Hi—I'm—um, I'm here to see Dr. Mush? Please?" Shamrock thought that was the hardest thing he would ever have to say. He had never been so nervous before in his whole life. It felt like the whole village was watching him.

"Oh. Sure," the gnome with the guitar said. Shamrock wondered if lots of creatures came to the village to ask Dr. Mush for help with the Gardener's Curse. "Just follow the path there, the one by the big purple mushroom, to the village garden. It's huge, so you can't miss it. The doctor should be there."

Shamrock wondered how he would find the scientist in the huge garden, but he just nodded and said, "Thank you for your help."

Village life started up again as Shamrock walked toward the big purple mushroom. He hoped his path to the doctor wouldn't be as long and scary as his path through the forest. Especially since his friends weren't with him anymore.

Shamrock sighed, thinking about how he had run away from his friend when she'd needed him. It was just that he needed help too. Comet had to understand that, right?

The path turned out not to be too long after all. Shamrock soon arrived at a walled garden. Stones had been piled up to about Shamrock's knees to form a rock wall that ran around a space filled with twisting plants, trees with fruit of every color, and flowers bursting out from every corner. Shamrock couldn't help but smile at it all. He pushed through the wooden gate in search of Dr. Mush. He couldn't wait to get rid of his curse.

"Hello?" Shamrock said as he walked through the garden. "Dr. Mush? Hello?"

Shamrock kept calling but no one answered. He walked deeper into the garden, through a little grove of lemon trees, and spotted a pointy red hat peeking over some flower bushes.

Shamrock ran over. "Dr. Mush!" He was so excited that

it came out much too loudly, and the gnome jumped up, his red hat flying off his head.

"Oh!" the gnome gasped with surprise. He picked up his hat, brushed it off, and put it back on his head. "Well, yes. I am Dr. Mush. But there's really no need to shout."

Shamrock cleared his throat. "I'm Shamrock, sir," he squeaked out, "and I have the Gardener's Curse, and I was hoping you could help me?" The words rushed out of him all in one breath.

Dr. Mush gave him a friendly, understanding smile. "Follow me, Shamrock. I think I can help."

Shamrock exhaled, relieved. He felt happier than he had in weeks! He followed the doctor through the garden. They ducked under some long willow tree branches that were touching the ground, making a sort of tent in the center of the garden. A large tree stump was underneath, with other little stumps around it, set up like a table and chairs. A teapot and teacups were in the center of the table, along with a big pile of biscuits.

"I was about to sit down for tea," Dr. Mush explained as he went over to the tea table. "I was just getting some lemons when you found me." Dr. Mush pulled out two lemons from his vest pocket and carefully started slicing them.

Shamrock bounced on his hooves. He didn't want to be rude, but he didn't have too much time before he had to head back to Unicorn University. His stomach did a little flip when he thought about going back through the forest, but he pushed that away and focused on the doctor.

"Tea?" the doctor asked, looking up after finishing cutting the lemon.

"No, thank you," Shamrock replied, thinking that he

would just knock over such a small, delicate teacup.

"Biscuit?" The doctor offered a little tray of blueberry biscuits.

Shamrock nodded and quickly gobbled a few of the tiny treats. He realized how hungry he was. He never had ended up eating those chocolates he'd brought—he had been too focused on getting to the village.

"Now, why in the five kingdoms do you think you have the Gardener's Curse?" Dr. Mush asked. He had settled down onto one of the small tree stumps and picked up his teacup and saucer. He looked at Shamrock over his half-moon glasses.

Shamrock took a deep breath. *Now or never*, he thought.

"Well, I love science, you see, and usually I'm really good at it," Shamrock started.

Dr. Mush nodded, his bright blue eyes twinkling with encouragement.

"But Garden Science class is different. I just feel a little out of place. Everything is messy, and, um, following directions and studying doesn't seem to be enough."

"Go on," Dr. Mush said.

"Professor Jazz gave me your journal, and it was so inspiring. I felt like you were the type of scientist I want to be, and, and—I wanted to grow the Golden Rose just like you. And prove to everyone that I wasn't behind in class, and get an A-plus. But, well, it turns out I couldn't grow the Golden Rose. I couldn't even grow a seedling. And I think I have the curse, the one you mentioned in your journal." Shamrock hung his horn. It was hard to tell the whole truth, but he felt better now that he had.

He peered at Dr. Mush, but neither one said anything for a long time. Dr. Mush nodded as if he were deep in thought.

Then Dr. Mush looked up and smiled. "I think the first thing I should say is that just because one class doesn't come naturally to you, it doesn't mean you are a bad student or that you should ever give up. It just means you need to work a little differently than maybe you normally do."

Shamrock felt confused. He *would* be great at Garden Science and get an A+, once he got rid of the curse.

"Then the next thing I should tell you is that there's no such thing as the Gardener's Curse. I made it up when I myself couldn't get the Golden Rose to grow and I was frustrated."

Shamrock's jaw dropped with surprise. *No such thing as the Gardener's Curse?* Shamrock couldn't think of one thing to say. He had made such a long journey! He'd broken a huge school rule and abandoned his friends when they'd needed him. All for nothing? He felt like he might be sick. Then he realized what the doctor had said about growing the Golden Rose.

"Wait, you couldn't grow the Golden Rose either?" Shamrock whispered. Had the doctor lied in his journal?

Dr. Mush shook his head. "You see, *I* couldn't grow the Golden Rose, but *we*—my fellow villagers and I—could."

Shamrock could only stare back. He was so very

confused. And his tummy was doing backflips.

"Here, here. Follow me, young unicorn." Dr. Mush put down his teacup and motioned for Shamrock to follow him deeper into the garden. They passed rows of tangled grapevines and groups of shrubs full of bright berries. They ducked under twisting green branches and walked around large leaves that had grown into the sunlight on the passageway. Soon they reached a clearing. When Shamrock looked up, he could see a giant golden flower that was three times the size of him growing in the center of the clearing.

Shamrock knew in his heart that this was the Golden Rose. It really did shine as if it were made from sunshine. It took Shamrock's breath away.

"You did do it!" Shamrock exclaimed.

"No, no, my whole village did it, and does do it. You see, no one can grow the Golden Rose alone. It says it right there in my directions!"

Luckily, Shamrock had brought his schoolbag with him

and could pull out the directions. He had read them so many times that he knew them by heart, so he knew they didn't say anything about that. He handed the book to Dr. Mush.

"No, it doesn't, Doctor!" Shamrock said defensively. "I always follow directions."

The doctor shook out the paper and brushed it off with his sleeve. "Aha!" he exclaimed. "Right here, on the side. It was covered with dirt. 'You'll need help.'"

Dr. Mush pointed to the margin, and Shamrock could see the line scribbled on the side. There were smudges of dirt around it. "How could I have missed it? I read the directions so many times!"

Dr. Mush nodded. "I'm just the same. Sometimes I can get in my own way—especially when I'm trying to prove something. The best advice I can ever give is in that margin—you should always ask for help! Especially with gardening. Creatures have been growing things since the very beginning of our world. And we ourselves have been able to grow and change so much because we shared our secrets—and our worries."

Shamrock nodded and thought back to what Stella had said earlier in the day. "I know, I know. That's why I'm here. I already looked through all the gardening books, so I knew that Professor Jazz couldn't help, and Professor Grub just told me to grow something else or talk to a classmate. You were the only other option."

Dr. Mush scratched his beard and scrunched his eyebrows. "Hmm, sounds like you were asking for help but not really listening."

Shamrock opened his mouth to argue, but he realized that Dr. Mush was right. Shamrock had been too proud to ask a classmate for help or even try a new flower. And he hadn't really asked Professor Jazz. He'd just decided the librarian couldn't help, before ever giving him a chance. Shamrock blushed with shame. He had gotten his friends to break school rules and get hurt, all because he had been too proud to really listen. "You're right, Doctor. I didn't really listen. I just always thought I knew best, even when I thought I was asking for help."

"That's what I thought," Dr. Mush said, looking at Shamrock. "But to grow the Golden Rose, you have to work with your community, and everyone has to listen to each other and work together. Each Golden Rose is different, and only a team can help it grow. And then you can work together to create something beautiful."

"I think I get the idea, but I still don't understand *why* you need more than one person to grow the Golden Rose."

"Ah! Yes, I'll explain," the doctor told him. "But why don't I explain on the way back to Unicorn University, eh?"

"You mean you'll come with me?" Shamrock's heart soared at the idea of not having to face the dark forest alone.

"How else can I show you the shortcut?" Dr. Mush winked at him.

Shamrock groaned. First no curse, and now he didn't even have to go through the scary forest? Shamrock had made some not-great decisions today. He hoped he wouldn't be in too much trouble when he got back.

Together Dr. Mush and Shamrock left the gnome village. Instead of going into the forest, they climbed into Dr. Mush's magical rowboat and glided down the Bubbling Brook. The sun was shining so brightly that the water glittered as the boat guided itself to Unicorn University. Shamrock smiled as he listened to Dr. Mush explain the magic of the Golden Rose. Shamrock didn't feel cursed anymore. Not one bit.

10

Coming Clean

"Ready?" Dr. Mush asked Shamrock outside the library. Shamrock sighed. "Ready."

Together the gnome and the unicorn walked up the Crystal Library's glittering steps to see Professor Jazz.

"Mush!" Professor Jazz called out when he saw them walk through the doors. "Shamrock! How wonderful that you two have met."

Dr. Mush raised his bushy white eyebrows at Shamrock. *Time to come clean.*

"Well, actually, Professor . . ." Shamrock pawed the floor

with his hoof a few times before looking up at the librarian. "I went looking for Dr. Mush in the gnome village because I thought I had the Gardener's Curse."

"Huh?" Professor Jazz seemed very puzzled. "What's the Gardener's Curse?"

"It's something I made up in my journal when I was having trouble with the Golden Rose," Dr. Mush explained.

"I read about it and thought I had the curse and that was why I couldn't grow anything in Garden Science class," Shamrock added.

Professor Jazz nodded and smiled with understanding. "I think I understand. You could have come to me, Shamrock. I could have helped you with this."

"I know—or I know that now," Shamrock said. "I just wanted to prove to everyone that I could get better at garden science on my own. But I see that's silly now."

Professor Jazz tapped his hoof a few times on the crystal floor. "Well, I guess you know what I have to do now."

Shamrock gulped, remembering that he could get in big, big trouble. Would he get expelled from the school? He'd never been so scared before. Not even in the forest!

"Since you came right to me and told me the truth, and if you promise to never leave school grounds again—" Professor Jazz started.

"I won't! I promise, Professor!" Shamrock squeaked.

"Then, as a punishment for breaking the rules," Professor

Jazz said, "you can put away all these books while Dr. Mush and I have a cup of tea and a chat."

Shamrock smiled. Spending the day in the library didn't sound like punishment at all. "Thank you, Professor!"

"Don't thank me yet, Shamrock," Professor Jazz said, and he and Dr. Mush walked away.

Shamrock turned back to the library and could see what he meant. There were stacks and stacks of books everywhere! There wasn't one table in the library that didn't have a pile of books on it, waiting to be put away. Shamrock didn't know how he would ever finish. His jaw hung open as he looked around, frozen in place.

Then he saw Twilight, Comet, and Sapphire walking toward him. Comet's hoof was wrapped in a bandage, and she walked with a little limp, but seemed okay.

"Hey, guys," Shamrock said softly when they reached him. "I'm really sorry I left you in the forest. Are you okay, Comet?"

Comet nodded, her eyes sparkling with mischief. "That was some adventure."

The four of them laughed together, and Shamrock knew that his friends had already forgiven him.

"Well, my punishment for leaving school is to shelve all these books." Shamrock pointed his horn around the room and sighed. "I don't think I'll ever finish."

Then he remembered Dr. Mush's advice. *Always ask for help.*

He looked up at his friends, his bushy eyebrows arching above his glasses. "Would you mind helping?"

"Of course we'll help!" the three of them said together, each smiling back at their friend.

"I mean, I'll sit over here and yell directions," Comet told them. "I have this sprained ankle, you see."

They all laughed and walked over to the closest table with a big pile of books. Shamrock's punishment didn't seem so bad anymore, now that he had help.

11

The Golden Rose

A few weeks later Shamrock hopped out of bed, more excited than he had ever been. Today was the big day!

He walked to the greenhouse, waving to classmates on the way.

"See you soon, Shamrock!" Peppermint called out.

Shamrock waved back. His cheeks hurt from smiling so much. He passed by the greenhouse and went right to the class garden. It was warm, and the sun was shining high in the sky. The air was breezy, and flowers were blooming all around him. But it wasn't just any old flower he was there to see.

Soon the rest of the Garden Science class arrived for the Golden Rose presentation. And they were giving the presentation together as a group to show Professor Grub how they had managed to grow one of the most impressive plants in the five kingdoms—by working together and following Dr. Mush's advice.

When everyone was gathered, Shamrock noticed that Dr. Mush and Professor Jazz stood with Professor Grub.

"We couldn't miss the big reveal!" Dr. Mush said when he caught Shamrock's eye.

The class had hung up a sheet for the occasion, so it would look like they were revealing a special painting or statue. Shamrock had to admit, the flower did look like a work of art.

Shamrock started off the presentation. "No one can grow

a Golden Rose alone. Each step in the process required help from other creatures."

Twilight stepped up next and said, "First you need to pack the soil with three *different* hooves. Each using a little different pressure."

Then Comet stepped up. "Then we used four different fertilizers. One of them was my grandmother's!"

Then Peppermint stepped up. "When the seedling sprouted up, we planted it next to my Rainbow Rose. And together the plants made each other stronger."

All the other students went on to explain how they had helped the process, and how the plant had grown as they'd worked together.

"And now it's time to share the results!" Sapphire said. "Shamrock, we all think you should do the honors."

Shamrock beamed. He walked over and pulled the sheet down to reveal the Golden Rose. It wasn't quite as big as the one in the gnome village, but to Shamrock it was even more beautiful.

As he looked at the rose, Shamrock could only think about all the little moments that had made it happen. From the frustrating ones, like when they hadn't been able to figure out why the seedling wasn't getting any bigger, to the surprising ones, like when someone had suggested they move the seedling outside and it had worked. Shamrock realized it was the journey that had made the flower so beautiful, and the fact that he'd gotten to share it all with his class. Even if the Golden Rose started drooping tomorrow, it would all have been worth it. Plus, they could figure out how to make it grow again. By working together.

Comet's Royal Cake

Comet flew through the air, feeling the cool wind on her pink cheeks. She dove and flipped over, her short blond hair whipping around her as she giggled with delight.

"Be careful!" Comet's grandmother shouted from below, where she was flying gracefully in between the tree trunks. Comet always thought Grandmother looked like she was swimming with the wind when she flew. Her soft blue cape never seemed to move out of place as she glided.

It's a pretty way to fly, Comet thought. . . . *Pretty boring!* Comet launched into another dive, skidding across the tops of the trees, making the branches flutter beneath her hooves.

It was winter, and all the leaves had fallen to the ground, leaving only spindly branches reaching up to the bright blue skies.

Comet and her grandmother were traveling to the capital for the Sunshine Springs Junior Baking Competition. Four foals from different schools were going to compete at the castle, and Princess Luna was even a judge. Comet had won a competition at Unicorn University against a student from Glitterhorn College, which had gained her entry into the royal competition, and now she was flying to the heart of Sunshine Springs. She could hardly believe it was real! Plus, as if baking for a *princess* weren't cool enough, Comet was even going to stay in the castle. She'd spent time in the capital before but had never stepped foot in the castle.

Comet did a little twirl in the air. She felt like a character from a book. This was the start of a grand adventure!

"Comet, look!" Grandmother called from below.

Comet glanced ahead to see the triangle tops of a castle appear in the distance. She could see flags perched at the tips of the buildings, flapping in the wind and practically touching the clouds.

And then something magical happened. It started to snow! Comet's heart filled with joy as glittering white snowflakes fell all around. She blinked as they caught in her eyelashes, making the world seem covered in sparkles. Comet couldn't remember ever being so happy.

This was going to be the best baking competition ever!

Before Comet knew it, they had reached the entrance to the city. With a giant spray of snow, she landed on the cobblestone street just before the open gates.

Comet's grandmother shook her head as she glided to a stop next to Comet. "You know, dear, if you practiced your landing as often as you practiced your flying tricks, you'd have a much smoother landing by now."

"But tricks are so much fun, and landings are *boring*. I'd rather just stay in the sky for as long as possible and only land once!" Comet shook the snow out of her mane and grinned.

Grandmother arched her eyebrows in response, but Comet saw her little smile, too.

"Anyway, today is the day for adventure—not practice!" Comet told her. She trotted away toward the castle gates, her hooves making a crunching sound as she pranced over the snowy cobblestone street.

Inside the gates there were unicorns everywhere! Some were milling about and window-shopping in front of the stores lining the streets, while others were selling sweets and newspapers out of stalls. There was a bookshop that, from what Comet could see through the door, was filled with books of every size. The city was just like Comet remembered, but better. And now that the city was covered in sparkling snow, it seemed like it was coated in white frosting. A perfect setting for a baking competition!

Up ahead she could see a crowd of unicorns standing

outside her uncle's bakery. Comet had worked there over the summer and knew there were always dozens of unicorns lined up waiting for her uncle's famous cookies. Comet went right toward the shop, excited to get a cookie of her own.

"Not now, Comet," Grandmother called from behind her. "We don't have time to stop by today. We're expected at the castle."

As delicious as a warm cookie would have been right then, Comet's heart soared at her grandmother's words. She was right. They were expected at the castle! *What a grand adventure.*